The
PROUD TREE

The PROUD TREE

Written by **Luane Roche**

Illustrated by **Chris Sharp**

LIGUORI
PUBLICATIONS
One Liguori Drive
Liguori, MO 63057-9999
(314) 464-2500

Copyright © 1995 and 1981, Liguori Publications
ISBN 0-89243-768-5

Library of Congress Catalog Number: 94-79668
Printed in United States of America

He was the straightest and sturdiest tree in the whole forest. Oh, but he was proud—too proud. "I'm the greatest," he would boast. "I'm as straight and sturdy as a Roman soldier, as brave as a centurion."

All the other trees grew tired of his constant bragging. They named him Rex (which means king) because he always acted and talked as if he were the king tree of all the forest.

Every morning at dawn and each evening at sunset, the trees of the forest would raise their branches in praise and thanks to God, their creator.

But not Rex. Rex was usually too busy admiring his own green leafy branches glistening in the morning sun or waving in the evening breeze.

One day some Roman soldiers from
Jerusalem came riding through the forest.
As they passed each tree, they would stop and
look the tree over carefully. Then they would
shake their heads and move on.

They came to a stop right in front of Rex.

Rex straightened his trunk and waved his powerful branches in the breeze. The leader of the soldiers climbed down from his horse and walked around Rex. He nodded his head and smiled.

"This tree will be perfect for the King," he said.

"The King?" Rex wondered. "What King? And why are they laughing?"

The soldiers circled Rex, feeling his rough bark, measuring his height, and nodding their heads.

"I must be the greatest tree in this forest for them to choose me for the King," Rex said out loud. "I hope all those other trees are watching and listening." He glanced around, smiling proudly.

"Maybe the King wants my beautiful branches for shade after his long trips from Rome," he thought. "Or maybe he is going to plant me in the palace garden for all his subjects to admire."

Rex could almost see himself in the royal
garden, with rare and colorful birds nesting
in his topmost branches.

Rex was excited. The very thought of being
the King's tree made him tremble all over.

But no! It was not from excitement that Rex was trembling. It was the soldiers. What were they doing to him?

Rex could feel the powerful blows of the soldiers' axes against his trunk. Whack! whack! went the axes.

Oh, no! They were cutting him down!

Rex screamed, "Don't! You can't do this to me. I will die if you cut me down. Don't you know who I am? I'm Rex—the king tree of all the forest. Stop this minute!"

He was too late.

With a great thundering sigh and a loud thud, Rex came crashing to the ground. His lovely branches were spread out on the forest floor. They would never wave in the breeze again. He had been cut away forever from the roots that gave him life.

No tree can live long without his roots. Rex would be dead in three days.

The soldiers cut Rex's trunk in two parts.
A short pole cut from his top was laid beside
him. They stripped away his branches and
leaves and trimmed off his bark.

Rex felt naked and very, very angry.

"How dare they treat me this way!"

The next thing Rex knew, both parts of his trunk were being chained to the soldiers' horses. They dragged him over bumps and rocks and through creeks—all the way to Jerusalem. When they finally came to a stop, they were in some sort of courtyard.

Workmen came along then and cut notches in each part of Rex's trunk. They fitted them together and tied them firmly in place.

"Well," thought Rex, "at least I'm all in one piece again."

Rex looked up at the sun. The sun was high in the sky. Rex knew it was late morning.

"Hey! I can see my shadow on the courtyard wall. Just look at that! They have shaped me into some kind of sign. A great surprise for the King, I'll bet."

Rex knew that something very special was about to happen. He could feel it in his trunk.

Through the open courtyard gates, Rex could see people lining up along the side of the road.

"This must be a very important event. And just think, I'm to be a part of it. It's too bad the other trees can't see me now. Boy, would they be jealous!"

Rex was almost glowing with his pride by now. He kept wondering when the King would come.

Suddenly, there was a great commotion in the courtyard. A man wearing a crown of sharp thorns was being pushed roughly into the yard by the soldiers. Blood trickled down the man's face and into his long hair. He had whip marks all over his body.

Rex wondered what this man could possibly have done that would make people treat him so badly.

"He looks so weak and beaten," Rex thought. "Yet, there is a regal look on his face—as if he were a King. Oh, no! This couldn't be the King the soldiers were talking about. It couldn't be. Who would treat a King like this?"

The soldiers were leading the man over to Rex. They grabbed Rex's trunk and laid it across the bleeding back of the man with the crown of thorns.

Rex felt himself being lifted—gently, almost lovingly.

Slowly the man began to carry Rex. They walked out of the courtyard, right down the street lined with people.

They headed toward a hill in the distance. It seemed such a long way to Rex.

All along the road, as Rex and the man passed by, people were watching. Some shouted angry words at them. Some laughed. Some were crying. Others just watched silently, without a word.

Three times the man fell before the soldiers finally grabbed someone from the crowd to help him.

"Well, it's about time," muttered Rex. "It took two horses to get me here, and they expect this man to carry me all the way up this hill alone."

At the top of the hill, there were two other trees shaped just like Rex.

"Lay the cross down here," a soldier growled. He turned to the other soldiers standing around. "This cross is to go in the middle."

"Cross!" thought Rex in surprise. "So that's what they made of me. This is a strange ceremony. But I'm going to be in the middle. That means I'm the star attraction."

All the people who had lined the road were beginning to gather at the top of the hill. The soldiers were tearing off the clothes of the man with the crown. The people were screaming at him. Suddenly, Rex felt more frightened than he had ever felt before.

"This isn't a very nice ceremony," he thought. "I'm beginning to wish I weren't a part of it."

The man with the crown of thorns was on his knees beside Rex.

"I've never seen eyes like this man's," Rex thought. "They are so gentle and kind—soft but so very, very sad."

Rex remembered how good it had felt to be carried by this man. After the cruel treatment the proud tree had received at the hands of the soldiers, being lifted onto those powerful shoulders had been like going back home to the forest comfortable and warm.

"How strange," Rex thought then. "He doesn't even seem angry at what these soldiers have done to him."

Rex's wondering was jolted by the sound of metal against metal. What were the soldiers doing now?

Suddenly he realized—they were nailing the man's hands and feet to Rex's trunk.

Rex could hardly believe this was happening. The man's warm blood ran from his wounds, soaking Rex's trunk. Rex felt sick.

The soldiers nailed a sign above the man's head. Then they raised Rex and the man upright. They planted Rex firmly between the other two crosses.

Rex whispered to the tree on his right, "What does the sign say?"

The answer startled Rex. The other tree whispered. "The sign says:"

**Jesus of Nazareth
King of the Jews**

Rex didn't have time to think. The crowd was getting loud and noisy. They shouted at Jesus and mocked him.

"If you are God, come down off that cross!" some yelled.

"He can save others, but he can't save himself," said others.

"Some King! Where's your army?" The voices were getting angrier and angrier.

"Son of God, where is your Father now?"

"God?" Rex said. He was so startled he almost shouted. "This can't be God. Look at what he has let them do to him. I can feel him struggling. His muscles twitch and cramp with the pain from his wounds. My trunk is soaked with his blood. I can hear him gasp when the pain gets bad. How can he be God?

"God is a Spirit, isn't he?"

As if in answer to his wondering, Rex heard Jesus speak. What he said sent shivers up and down Rex's trunk.

"Father, forgive them. They do not know what they are doing." Jesus' voice was gentle and pleading.

Rex was stunned!

"Don't know what they're doing? Forgive them? Are you going mad with your pain? Nobody forgives people like this. Even trees don't forgive such terrible cruelty. All creation knows we have to hate our enemies! Especially when they beat us and put us to death."

Rex kept trying to reason with Jesus. After all, the man on the cross had every reason in the world to be angry.

"Listen, nobody ever forgives people like this," he said again. "Nobody, of course, except maybe G—O—D!"

Suddenly, Rex realized who this man was. He began to feel weak.

Rex began to stammer. "Who—who did he call Father? I have heard talk of a Father in heaven—and a Son. Could this really be God? Can it be that this is truly the Father's Son?"

The very thought filled Rex with wonder. "He—he's touching me. He carried me. He is nailed to me. Why would God want to be so close to me?"

Sadly, Rex spoke to Jesus. "I really haven't been a very nice tree. To be honest, I am probably the worst of all the trees in the forest. There are other far better trees that you could be nailed to. Why me, Jesus? Why me of all the good and loyal trees?"

Rex began to weep thick, sticky sap.

"I'm sorry that I have never been a tree your Father could be proud to say he created. I'm really, really sorry."

Sap ran from all parts of Rex's trunk. It coated the ground and mingled with the blood streaming from the wounds of Jesus.

Rex heard Jesus speak once more. His voice sounded far away. Jesus said: "Father, into your hands I entrust my Spirit."

Then Rex felt the body of Jesus sag in a dead weight. A powerful sadness filled Rex's heart.

It was still early afternoon. Heavy black
storm clouds gathered in the sky. The clouds
covered the sun, turning day into night.

The rumble of thunder shook the earth with
its angry voice. Bolts of lightning darted across
the sky, pointing accusing fingers of light at all
the people on earth.

The crowd was restless and fearful. They
kept looking up at the sky, then at one another,
then at Jesus. One by one, people began to drift
away.

Rex watched the crowd disappear, robes
pulled up over their heads. He thought they
looked like thieves running from the scene

of a crime. The violent wind pushed at their
backs. A torrent of rain soaked through their
clothing.

Then the crowd was gone. Rex saw two silent figures below the cross. There was the woman Jesus had called Mother. Beside her was the young man who had been his friend.

Rex shook his trunk ever so gently. "Jesus," he called. There was no answer.

"Jesus," he called a little louder. There was still no answer, no movement from the man on the cross.

Rex's voice became anxious. "Wake up! Wake up, Jesus!"

Now Rex was yelling. "I said I'm sorry!"

Terror gripped at Rex's heart. He screamed, "I'm sorry! Please, Jesus, forgive me too! Don't die!"

The figure on the cross remained absolutely silent. "How can this be?" Rex asked. "You are God! God can't die!"

There is an old story about trees that are dying. The story goes like this. If a dying tree tells God he is sorry for the bad things he has done, if he wishes he had been better, God will give him *new life* from one of the tree's own seeds.

Rex knew that he had been proud and ungrateful all his life. He wanted Jesus to hear how sorry he was. But Jesus was silent now. Rex thought to himself, "He can't hear me. I've lost my chance to have new life."

Rex wanted God to know that he was grateful for the honor of being chosen for this day.

"I want to thank God for coming so close to me," he prayed silently. "I want to raise my branches in praise of his goodness. Oh, but I can't do that now. I have no branches left. I am naked and alone. It's too late."

Rex turned very pale. It was indeed too late. The centurion had just stabbed Jesus in the side with a long lance.

Blood and water ran from the wound.

Jesus was dead!

Rex remembered the story about dying trees. It is said that a tree hears music just before he dies.

If the music is sad and very depressing, the tree will never have new life.

But...if the music is like angels singing praise to God—like an Alleluia—the tree will have a new growth grander than the first.

"I wish Jesus could have heard me before he died," Rex said. "If only he had known how much I loved him—how sorry I am for being proud.

"I never gave a thought to the needs of others. I wanted everything for myself. I thought

I was the best, the first. I thought I was a self-made tree.

"If only I had thanked my Creator. If only I had loved my neighbor. I should have told Jesus sooner."

But Jesus was gone now. His friends had come and carried his body away. The trees had watched them go. The wind voices told Rex that Jesus had been buried in a borrowed tomb carved out of rock. Guards were posted outside the entrance to make sure Jesus stayed inside.

"That's pretty silly," said Rex. "Where could a dead person go?"